FAMILY BETRAYAL: THEY FAKED GRANDMA'S TEXTS

by Nia Zola

from: **Very Rich Stories**

https://www.youtube.com/@VERYRICHSTORIES

ISBN: 978-1-967860-41-8

Papereback Version

Table of Contents

FAMILY BETRAYAL: THEY FAKED GRANDMA'S TEXTS

Who Would Believe It?

My family, if I can call them that now, faked Grandma's texts... just to steal my inheritance. For years, they pretended Grandma was alive, but she was not. This was significant because Grandma left me an inheritance which they kept and spent. They kept pretending that Grandma was alive while they spent my money.

I always knew my family could be a little selfish. I always knew my mother played favoritism toward my brother Melvin, but I never thought she – or they'd stoop this low. They didn't just take my inheritance. They didn't just lie to my face, they kept me away, so they never saw my face and I didn't see theirs, for years. And for those years, they didn't even tell me... that my grandma — the one person I thought had my back — was gone.

I was hundreds of miles away, busting my butt in college, thinking Grandma was still alive. She was sending me sweet little texts, dropping me small amounts of money to help me out from time to time. I had no idea those messages weren't coming from her.

Shortly after I had arrived for my first semester at university, my grandma was already dead, and I did not know it. And my family — my own parents — decided not to tell me. They hid it from me.

My grandma and I were super close. It was Grandma that I had the hardest time leaving when I accepted my full academic scholarship to college, a few states away. All the while the people who allegedly gave birth to me—but never really acted like it, must have really wanted me gone. And it seems they disrespected Grandma and wanted her gone too.

Why?

So, they could take everything she left me. And spend it on themselves… and my brother.

They took everything — including Grandma.

I would never have imagined that my own mother would have been this heartless to lie to and steal from her own daughter like that.

Thank God for my cousin, Jasmine for letting me know what was going on back home and helping me find the truth.

Off to School

So… I went to college a few states away on an academic scholarship. Sounds great, right? Except, the scholarship didn't cover everything. I still had fees, books, and living expenses. And guess what? My family wasn't exactly lining up to help me out. It was humiliating, every time I asked for financial help from home, I was turned down.

At first, I figured they were just giving me space. But every time I said I wanted to come home for a visit — even for holidays — they'd say, 'Oh, it's too expensive,' or 'It's not a good time.' It started feeling weird, like they really didn't want me there.

The one person on my side? My grandma. She'd text me these sweet little messages, sometimes even send me $50 or $100 here and there. Honestly, it felt like she was the only one rooting for me. Whether she sent money or not, hearing from Grandma really made my day and kept me focused on my goal. I needed those words of encouragement, and I promised myself that I would make her proud.

Okay, I thought going to college was supposed to be this huge, life-changing opportunity. And for a minute, it kinda was. I got a scholarship —, full ride, but only for tuition. Everything else? I was on my own. And apparently… my family made sure I stayed on my own. Grandma and I had a beautiful relationship based on a real person to person connection; it was not based on money. Growing up, it never occurred to me that she had a lot of money; I didn't think of her like that. Grandma didn't make our relationship about money; it was about quality time spent together; it was about love and respect. For that reason, I never thought to bypass my parents by asking Grandma for money, but when she sent it, I was thankful and grateful.

School of Business

College was three states away, but I never thought it was optional – not with my hard-earned GPA. I had to get my college degree. I was always interested in business not for the sake of earning money, but for the excitement of commerce, for the sake of business itself, for the creativity and for being able to supply needs, goods, and services for people.

But I didn't realize how expensive UVA would be. fees, books, rent... life. And my family? Every time I'd hint at needing financial help, they'd shut it down. I didn't even know why I had to even ask; I'm a student for goodness sake.

Their replies, mostly when I talked to my mother over the phone were things like, *'We don't have it right now,'* or *'It's good for you to be independent.'* Even when I wanted to come home for holidays, they'd make up excuses. 'Oh, travel's too expensive…' *'We've got a lot going on…'"* Wow, my own family giving me the brush off. This hurt. Then I'd try to be more grown up and rationalize, maybe they were busy. I mean, life happens, right? I tried to believe that.

The one person who made me feel like I wasn't totally alone? My grandma. She'd text me little notes like, 'Proud of you,' 'Keep going, Emily. That was stuff that actually made me feel seen. And every now and then, she'd send me a few dollars, saying, 'Get yourself something nice.' Honestly, it kept me going, some days.

She had done that same thing when I was in high school too. I had the sweetest Grandma. That was for the first two years of college. While at college, earning my degree, I noticed during the holidays and at certain times for a week or 10 days at a time, the messages and encouragement money seemed to slow down to less than a trickle. There were weeks, especially in the summer, when it seemed to nearly dry up. Then it would suddenly pick back up. I thought that was odd. I thought maybe Grandma was tired or forgot about me or something. I hoped she was feeling fine, and I wanted to go home and visit her. Of all the people back home, it was Grandma that I missed the most.

I'd text Grandma, but she wouldn't answer me for days. I chalked it up to old age. She always had a sharp mind, but time can take a toll on people. I would call her, but she can't hear even a little bit. You would know that if you went to her house and heard how loud she plays the TV.

It was sweet of her to send me anything, at all, although, even though up until that point it wasn't regular, and it didn't last.

During winter break, since I was almost always strapped for cash, both years, I stayed local and worked at my part time jobs. Because even if I went home, I may not find summer or temporary employment there. So, I stayed on campus. The first year when we had to vacate the dorms for winter break, Mrs. Richardson, who owned the coffee shop where I worked, had a niece in college, so I stayed at her niece's campus house during the winter break because all of the girls that lived in that house went home. They had normal families that wanted to see them. It was shocking to me that my family wasn't "normal." Perhaps they were fine with just having Melvin and didn't miss me at all. And when I didn't hear from Grandma it was nearly depressing since everyone needs family connections and emotional support, especially when they are away from home, *right?*

Melvin, Living Large

It was my cousin on my Dad's side of the family, Jasmine, who became emotional support for me, even while she spilled family tea. "Girl, you're away at college and I don't even think Melvin is working."

"Melvin? No, he probably isn't working. He is mom's pride and joy, and I don't know why – he needs to get in college or get a job or something."

Meanwhile, back home, my little brother — who, let's be real, wasn't exactly the family genius — was living it up.

"Melvin?" continues Jasmine, "Every time I see him, he's *dripping*. New clothes. Gold jewelry. I swear I saw 2 carat diamond studs in his ears. Private sports coaching."

"Yeah, Emily asserted, "like the NBA's going to draft him from his momma's couch."

"He'd have more of a chance if he was in college."

"Well, that's the truth, but Emily, they even bought Melvin a brand-new Jeep for his birthday."

"What?"

"Yup, that's like a $60,000 vehicle."

"Wow, Jazz, I'm sitting here working a bunch of part time jobs and keeping up with my studies, eating Ramen on a regular, and Melvin's living the life."

"Do you go on his socials?"

"No, not really, I don't have time, I've got my head in these books. I don't even have time to go on my own socials, and if I would see him bragging, it would just make me mad."

"Well, he's getting trips like it's nothing. Every month he's posting pictures like he's a vacation blogger or something."

"Like where is he going to?"

"Out of state, out of the country. Mexico. Costa Rica, Dominican Republic. He went to the Montreal Jazz Festival."

"Melvin doesn't even like jazz. That was probably an excuse to go to Canada."

"Yeah, maybe, but then next he was at the Newport Jazz Festival."

"He's a kid. What does he know about music?"

"Then we see him at a NASCAR race."

"What!"

"Emily, the pictures look legit.

"Jasmine, Cuz—I'm glad to catch up with you, but I've gotta go."

"Talk to you later. "

"Okay Bye."

Emily wasn't jealous. She was angry. She was hurt. She might have been furious. She thought about confronting them, but her mother could hear nothing against her precious Melvin. He could do no wrong, even when he was wrong and was standing in the kitchen with wrong in his hands. If he came in past curfew for his age, it didn't make a difference. If his grades sucked so bad that he couldn't get accepted to college – mostly because he didn't even go to class, their mother would just cover for him.

And the dad let their mother dote on him and paid little attention to the house but was always at work and working his businesses.

Thank God for Grandma

The only person who really seemed to have my back was my Grandma. She wasn't big on phone calls. They said it was her hearing had gotten worse since I had started college. So, it's not like I could call her and vent, but I sure did want to. Grandma almost never answered her phone, but she would text me sometimes. Encouraging texts like, *Emily, I know you will do well.* Sometimes she'd even send me a little money, like, *'Here, buy yourself something.'*

And honestly? Those texts and those tiny amounts of money? They got me through some pretty rough times that first year.

But then… things started feeling a little off. How could decent parents let their child be off at college and not give her any support – like none, at all? Did they not have a conscience?

Did they want me to suffer? Or were *they* really suffering?

If it weren't for Grandma I don't know how I'd make it. But things were odd, like, I'd text Grandma back with specific questions, and her responses would be super generic. Or I'd mention something I told her before, and she'd act like she'd never heard it. Once, I asked how her best friend and neighbor, Jane, was doing, and she totally ignored it.

I brushed it off. I mean Grandma was old. Maybe it was memory stuff? Sometimes Emily wished she had Jane's number so she could call her and get updates on Grandma. Yeah, that's what she'd do next time she was home, she'd get Jane's phone number since she lived right next door to Grandma.

What Emily didn't know is that Grandma loved her instantly--, her first grandchild. The moment she laid eyes on her that was it. Grandma loved Emily's sweet spirit and her intelligence. Grandma didn't miss her daughter Lumira cut her eyes at her own mother by Grandma's reaction to first seeing Emily. It was jealousy, bordering on evil. Lumira's husband was captivated with the little newborn, everyone was so excited. Lumira felt left out, forgotten, jealous. She had an instant grudge against her own daughter. How could she cover that up? It was careful play acting at first, but then she couldn't hide it anymore after her second child, her son, her golden child was born.

Melvin was born very soon after, and it was as though Lumira made the biggest deal over him as if to pay Emily back for being adorable and smart and getting all the attention. It became a war of sorts, the more time and attention Grandma gave Emily, the more attention Melvin got from his mother who soon recruited her husband to dote on Melvin and basically   ignore   Emily.

The irony was that the more attention Lumira gave Melvin, the more Grandma tried to make up the difference because that little girl hadn't done anything to deserve being ignored or treated poorly by her parents.

Deep inside, Grandma knew Lumira had a wicked spirit, and she secretly wished Emily was her real daughter instead of the one named Lumira. Even if Lumira didn't know this, she somehow sensed it. But it was by Lumira's own making, her own evil ways, not by anything Emily ever did.

Home For Summer?

I made it through second semester, with the very least amount of emotional family support of any college kid, like ever. Except for Grandma, I don't know how I would have made it. My own mother, Grandma's only child, was not a nurturing mother—at least not to me. She was the perfect mother to Melvin, I'm sure, but not to me. And, she was nothing like Grandma.

In spite of it all--, wow! I made it through the first year, even without going home for winter break and now I was going to be a sophomore in college in the fall. I called mom to let her know I'd be coming home, and could she arrange my flight and ticket home to Indiana?

Oh? She asked as if it was something foreign for a college kid to come home in the summer.

"Well, Mom, can you get me a ticket to fly home? Last day of classes is May 5th."

Mom stopped me saying, "You know honey how you stayed and worked during winter break? We don't have funds for you so you might as well stay the summer and work to—you know, to save up for next year's fees."

"But mom, I haven't been home in almost a year. I want to see everybody."

She wasn't listening to me at all. They didn't want me to come home? I felt so bad. I felt so ashamed that even with a full tuition scholarship that the family I was from was so poor they couldn't help me, or I couldn't' even take a break for Christmas or summer. I vowed within myself that when I finished college I must be in a position to help my family, so they don't suffer like I'm suffering right now.

It's so odd, though, I always thought we were middle class or even upper middle class. I never felt like we grew up poor, so I didn't understand why funds were so slack in my family. It was sobering. It was saddening. But hearing about and sensing this financial strain gave me the drive to push forward all the more and pursue my education and business dreams.

Yet in the back of my mind, I wondered how my brother Melvin was able to take so many trips. I whispered a sincere prayer: *Lord, I hope he's not doing anything illegal.*

Emily turned her mind back to work and reality, and survival, really and went to work for her usual afternoon shift.

After this horrible blow, Mrs. Richardson, who had become a surrogate mother to me, noticed my crestfallen face. She said, "You know Emily, one of the girls in the house where my niece lives has graduated, so there's a room there now if you would like to share the rental house with those girls. Each room has its own bathroom and privacy. It's pretty nice, actually. You will have full access to and use of the kitchen as well."

Wow! I needed friends. I needed companionship. I needed a family, more than anything else. But these girls were around my age – maybe we'd bond, and I'd have a "college family." That's when I   learned that Mrs. Richardson was able to make the offer because she owned the house and rented it to students every year.

So, I stayed the summer too. A couple of the other girls took summer classes, so I wasn't alone in the house.

Mrs. Richardson gave me more hours in the coffee shop. When school was closed for summer, I got a second job in a retail store, with that discount I could buy a few items of clothing for school. The rent for the room with access to the kitchen and the whole house was more affordable than the dorm with its included cafeteria fees.

Grandma's Recipe Box

One day that first summer of still being on campus, feeling exhausted and bummed out, I finally took out the recipe box that Grandma had given me when I first came to campus. She had told me, "Emily, these recipes are very important; never lose this box." Oh, I remembered the cookies Grandma and I baked at her house. They were delicious.

Grandma had said, "If you miss me, bake some cookies; they will do wonders for you."

Maybe Grandma was right. I opened the recipe box that I had brought from home and now that I was in a house and not in the dorm, I had a way to bake. Recipe cards were crammed in that box. There is no way we baked all those flavors of cookies. It's like Grandma stuffed the box on purpose.

As I lifted the lid to open the box, the entire box slipped and fell to the floor. Things scattered everywhere. Oh my goodness! There was a hundred-dollar bill attached to the back of every recipe card. Some weren't even recipe cards, just blank index cards stuffed in the back of the box, with a one-hundred-dollar bill attached to the back of each.

Grandma! I exclaimed.

I was so relieved. There was nearly $3000 crammed in that recipe box all that time. Tears filled my eyes and as I fumbled to separate the money from the recipe cards and put the recipes back in the box, I saw a small white bank envelope wedged in the bottom of the box. I opened it with trembling hands. Inside the envelope was 2000 dollars more in cash. Also inside the envelope was a little note. 'Sorry I had to stash the money like this, it's just that if your mother saw me giving you money, she probably wouldn't give you any.'

Oh, Grandma, she hasn't given me any anyway.

And, Emily kept reading, teary-eyed. 'Some people, whenever they see a wallet open they think it is open for them. You're a child and a student and I'm so proud of you. Grown people can get help for a while, but they must learn to stand on their own in time.

You know I don't hear well, Bunny, so we will have to make these texts keep us connected. Let me know when you need more money.

Love always, Grandma.'

Grandma!

I didn't bake cookies that day. With blurred, teary vision I put all the cookie recipes back in the box and just sat down. An hour later I was at the bank to put the money in my tiny account that held no more than 2 or 3 hundred dollars. Relieved.

I called Grandma, but the call went to voice mail--, again. I texted Grandma – Grandma, thank you, I finally can bake cookies again. They are so sweet, and so are you.

I sent her a selfie smiling in front of the bank. She'd know what I meant. Yeah, that was enough. I'd tell her more when I saw her in person. I had promised Mrs. Richardson that I'd work this summer, but maybe I'd have enough money to fly home for winter break this time or at least take the train.

I told Grandma that I moved from the dorm to a house with some other students and it was very affordable. She suddenly started sending me $250 a month almost like clockwork. Well, it was a bank transfer – I don't know how Grandma figured that out, maybe someone at the bank helped her.

At any rate, I texted her and thanked her. You know, a real card would be nicer. I started writing notes and cards to Grandma once a month when her benevolence hit my bank account, and usually just in time each month for rent. She sent half of my rent for the small room so I still had to work, but it was doable now.

Third semester was a little easier. I didn't feel so alone and made friends with the other girls in the house and in some of my classes. That house was amazing; it was big, with six ensuite bedrooms. It wasn't a new house, but it had been refurbished and restyled very well.

The Cookie Empire is Born

I didn't go home the second winter break or summer either. It was as though I had moved to that college town. It was welcoming. I had made friends, and Mrs. Richardson had been wonderful to me since the first day I met her.

One day I took a dozen cookies that I made from Grandmas' recipes to the coffee shop. Mrs. Richardson loved them and asked if I might consider making them for her coffee shop. I said, "Sure." I quit my second job and baked cookies all the time when I wasn't in class or studying. It was a joy, and the students were buying them not just individually, but by the handful and then by the bagful and then by the box full, a dozen at a time. It was funny, instead of the college kids getting cookies from home, the parents were requesting the kids send them cookies from college.

Mrs. Richardson had a small commercial kitchen in the coffee shop as they sold other baked goods, but the cookie sales took over. I baked every day so there was the fresh smell of cookies, flavor of the day – and coffee, it was intoxicating and there was a line every afternoon.

I learned so much about business from Mrs. Richardson. She didn't just have the coffee shop; she owned real estate that was very profitable since the students needed apartments.

I became interested in coffee and how it was sourced. I suggested to her that we could look for a direct source of coffee from Kenya and form a relationship with Kenyan women since they do most of the coffee growing there. Truthfully, it was a business model that I had seen on Shark Tank, but it really inspired me, and I was able to inspire Mrs. Richardson. Then I suggested to her that we could roast the coffee ourselves and offer it for sale by the bag, in the store.

You know Mrs. Richardson, these college kids stay up late nights studying when we are not open--, and they want—

Coffee! they both said together.

And what about you, Emily?

Me? Oh wow! It was so nice to have someone concerned about me. As my real part-time job I baked cookies every time I was not in class or studying. Sometimes I baked cookies while I was studying; I brought my books and laptop to the shop. I got 40% of cookie profits.

The cookies and coffee became so popular that I then said to her that we should set up a website. Mrs. Richardson was amazed at how much people love coffee and cookies and we began to double profits.

Using what I was learning in Darden, since I was a business major, I suggested to her that she should open another coffee shop in another college town. So, she did. She opened up coffee shops in neighboring college towns. One at JMU, Radford, Hampden Sydney and Longwood. Each one took off as if these kids never had coffee and cookies before. She got business majors to run the coffee shops and report to her. It was a fantastic business model.

This began her coffee shop, roasting, and selling empire. Mrs. Richardson was widowed and had no children, so we kind of adopted each other. Her niece and I remained friends, but she had her own parents, plus she was two years ahead of me and had graduated, gotten married and moved abroad, busy with her own life. This was different for Emily since she didn't have to compete with anyone for well-deserved mentoring or parental-type attention. It was exhilarating to be seen and heard and to be doing business successfully.

Mrs. Richardson started importing the Kenyan grown coffee directly from the source. She then found local coffee bean roasters and packagers. She also found and rented an automated commercial kitchen just for baking Grandma's cookies. Even though she loved baking, in order to scale the business, automation had to be used. After all the demand was rising and I'm not a cookie elf.

Before they started selling the packaged coffee and cookies, Mrs. Richardson said, "Emily, we have to name this brand and get logos designed."

You're right. Hmm, my Grandmother's name is Pearl, Pearl Donovan. I want to name the brand Miss Pearl's Cookies. And what about your coffee, Mrs. R?

Our coffee, Emily. Let's name it Richardson's Fine Roast. RFR. Yeah, they agreed on the names and shook hands like real business partners.

The orders began pouring in for Richardson's Fine Roast coffee and Miss Pearl's Cookies. Sometimes just for the coffee, sometimes just for cookies, but it was a growing empire. More staff was hired for fulfillment; the operation was growing. Emily was receiving a portion of the profits for the cookie sales and no longer had to worry about enough money for school expenses.

Emily couldn't wait to tell Grandma, but not her immediate family – she had a check in her spirit about them for some reason; she didn't know why.

But she soon would.

What Happened to Grandma?

So, it's two years into college at UVA and I'm on FaceTime with my cousin Jasmine one random night, just catching up, and she goes, "Hey did you see those vacation pix of your family?"

"No. what did they go to the mountains or something?"

"The mountains in Iceland."

"What! What do you mean Iceland? Black people don't go to Iceland."

"The Black people you're related to went there last summer. And Uncle Robert – your dad--, they went to actual Iceland."

"What?"

"Your family is traveling a lot. And Melvin is standing there cheesing in every picture. For Christmas last year they went to Santorini?"

"What! Santorini? Jasmine, are you making this stuff up?"

"No. I'm not making this up. It was their Christmas vacation. Hang on and I'll send you some screenshots. It's a shame you couldn't go for having to work an all."

"Jasmine, I didn't' have to work. Mom told me to stay here and work because they were too busy and they didn't have any money to help me with college expenses."

"Wait, wait, wait – they've got plenty of money."

"Well Jazz, my dad does okay in business, but they must be character building or something when it comes to me because they are not hooking me up on the regular."

"They don't help you?"

"No, every time I ask, things are tight or something. If it weren't for Grandma---"

Jasmine interrupted, "Emily, ever since your mother's mother died, they've been rolling in money."

"Grandma died? Grandma? Unintended sobs started and hot tears burned two lines down Emily's face."

"Emily," Jasmine dared to whisper, "you didn't know?"

"Oh Jazz, I did not know. This is impossible. Grandma didn't die. Stop playing with me; it's not funny."

"No Emily." Jasmine softened but said, "It's wild how your Grandma Pearl passed and all that money stuff.'"

And I'm like... "What? Passed? What do you mean... passed? She can't be gone, Jasmine. Grandma's alive. She just texted me last week. We've been keeping up by text ever since I got to college. I'll send you a screen shot of our thread."

Then she goes, "Wait... you really didn't know?'"

"Turns out... your Grandma, your mother's mother, passed your first semester at college, late October after you first started. I know how close you two were and I had thought that's why you didn't come back home because it was all too much for you. That's why I didn't bring it up before. I felt like it must have been too fresh for you."

"No. Jazz. I didn't know Grandma had - -, Emily didn't even want to say the word, but she did. I didn't know Grandma had died. Why didn't you tell me?"

"I figured your mother had told you. It's her mother after all."

"No. She hasn't said a word about her own mother."

"Jazz, are you sure that Grandma is gone?" Emily was still in disbelief, in the first stage of grief—denial. But then she said, "Jazz, I gotta go, this is too much for me right now."

"OK Emm, I'll check on you tomorrow, is that Okay?"

Emily sat on her couch all that night in absolute shock, forcing herself through the stages of grief, all in one night. She looked over the text messages from Grandma, they'd never really stopped, at least one or two a week since she entered college with some breaks every now and again. What is going on? she spoke, talking to herself. She wasn't imagining any of this, plus Grandma was sending money. Who was behind this?

None of this made any sense.

My family has been lying to me for months — no for *years*. They were cold hearted snakes. Living it up while I suffered, pretending to be Grandma--, my sweet Grandma. She was my champion. She believed in me. Now I felt extra alone and sick to my stomach. "Look what those people have done," she said aloud.

Without Grandma, did I even stand a chance now? How could I finish the last two years of this program? Who is going to be my emotional support now?

Emily just wept and wept all night.

Grandma Pearl

Two years ago, just after Emily left for university, when she saw the late summer sunlight glare off the roof of the sedan that parked in front of her neighbor and best friend's house, Jane pulled her curtain back slightly as she peered out the window of her brownstone to get a good look. It was Lumira, her neighbor's only child, Emily's mother, if you want to call her that. A couple hours later, she saw that same sedan pull off. If Jane's eyes weren't fooling her, and they usually didn't, she could have sworn she saw Lumira tucking an envelope into her purse, exchanging them for her car keys as she walked back to her vehicle.

She thought to herself, wonder what Lumira has taken now? Jane decided to go next door and visit Pearl and find out. Jane was curious because some weeks ago she had seen

Jane take Pearl's checkbook and was probably draining that account. Jane didn't trust Lumira and really neither did her mother, Pearl.

Jane had to knock several times. Pearl came to the door kind of wobbly and groggy. She was not herself, not by Jane's estimation.

"Oh Pearl, sit down," and helped Pearl back to the sofa. She said it twice, the second time facing Pearl so Pearl could read her lips. "Was that Lumira?"

"Yes, she came by."

"She hasn't been here in a week or more. They've been on vacation."

"She and her husband and that boy?"

"Melvin—."

"Yes, Melvin. They all went on an overseas trip."

"Where did they go?"

"She didn't say but she brought me this souvenir gift."

She pointed to a bird carving made of a very dark wood. It was now hanging on the wall. Jane thought it was atrocious, and it really gave her the creeps.

"This is *different*, Pearl. What did Lumira say this was?"

"Lumira gave it to me with a smile, like she was really proud of it, saying, *'Just a little something to watch over you when I can't be here.'*"

Pearl had put it on her mantle or side table, not realizing it's meant to "watch" in a very different way. Lumira went to the wall and took down a picture that was already hanging and put this atrocity up in its place.

"Oh wow, Pearl, it's really something," Jane said as she went over and took a good look at it. Then she said, "India? They went to India?"

"I think that's what she said, Jane."

"Why would they go to India?"

"I don't know. That girl is her father's child--, just like him. Lumira has always been *different*. That's the best way I can describe her.

More like her father than me and that's for sure."

"Oh well. Do you want me to help you with anything Pearl, or did Lumira do everything for you already? I see she made some tea."

"And, she changed the batteries in my hearing aid."

The two sat in silence for a while. Pearl seemed to be dozing off, so Jane suggested, "Okay, good, let me wash that teacup for you Pearl."

"No, Jane you don't have to, I can get it later, right now I feel sleepy and want to take a nap."

Jane washed the teacup and saucer, put the sugar away and basically snooped around the kitchen. There were a few sugar granules on the countertop and there were some very fine specks of some other light powder that didn't look like sugar. She took a picture of it with her cellphone. There were no batteries in the trash, there were no battery wrappers in the trash but there was a small box that said, Hearing Aid

Device in the trash. Before leaving, Jane took a few more pictures while Pearl napped. She said, "Pearl, I'll come check on you tomorrow." then she let herself out as Pearl stretched out on her couch for an afternoon nap.

Jane was troubled all night herself and had a weird dream of a flock of birds flying over. There were so many of them that they blocked the sun. Jolted awake, she got up, showered and got dressed and came back to see Pearl the next morning as she had promised. Pearl was feeling fine, just like herself again and was in the kitchen making coffee and toast. While she piddled at the coffee maker, Jane walked over and took a hard look at that souvenir Lumira had given her friend, Pearl yesterday. It was a wooden sculpture of a raven perched on a carved lotus flower. Inlaid with tiny red gemstones for the eyes that seem to glint in low light. The base was carved with intricate symbols.

Yes, Mumbai is full of witchcraft, Jane thought to herself. Now, I don't believe in all that, but people take trips to do suspicious things to other people. I can't even explain what this ugly thing is, but Jane was from New

Orleans and this thing looked kind of witchy to her.

Neither of them knew this but Lumira had been to a spiritualist in the dark streets of Mumbai to get this item, not for its beauty but for her own purposes. She wanted money from Pearl again and had run out of ways to ask for it or trick her mother out of it. She had even tried to get money from Grandma under the guise of sending it to Emily, but Grandma wasn't falling for that. She was planning to send Emily money directly every month.

By this time, Lumira's evil heart had convinced her that she shouldn't have to ask for it, wasn't it really her money already? Grandma wasn't going to live forever and Lumira wanted to be sure of that. And Lumira, as the only child knew—or hoped that Grandma would leave her everything, except for Emily. Lumira had already hatched the plan to keep Emily and Grandma apart. With Emily at college, Lumira was now making her moves.

Jane extended her hand to touch this thing, it felt bone chilling cold. Wood doesn't feel cold she thought to herself. The house isn't cold, it's still summer; it's not winter. The underside of the base has faint, oily residue from a ritual oil used during the Mumbai ceremony.

They sat down for a cup of coffee together. Pearl said, "I had some strange dreams when I napped yesterday. Then I went to sleep late last night and had the same dream again. It was odd, Jane.. I keep having a dream of that bird talking and laughing. The other night the bird was defecating in a cage, defecating small gold coins. It was bizarre."

"Pearl, I think a lot of things are weird. I dreamed of birds last night too."

"What? I didn't hear you."

"Pearl," said Jane raising her voice abnormally, "I think a lot of things are weird."

Pearl looked confused and touched her ear, she couldn't hear.

Jane looked in disbelief, the hearing aids with the fresh batteries just changed yesterday don't work today.

"Pearl, I'm going on an errand later Come with me and let's drop in to your audiologist and have him look at your hearing aids."

Pearl did not know what Jane was saying until Jane nearly shouted it from the rafters.

Dr. Wells, Audiologist

"These hearing aids don't work, Mrs. Donovan."

"Yeah, I know, that's why I came in here."

"Okay... did you drop them in water or something?"

"No," Grandma, confused, insists, "But... my daughter just changed the batteries yesterday."

Dr. Wells repeats, looking at Grandma so she can read his lips, "Mrs. Donovan, this isn't the device we prescribed."

"What!"

"They are damn close – excuse my language. They are almost an exact copy of the brand we prescribed but this is not my programming. These are not your hearing aids."

"What!"

"What happened to your real hearing aids, Mrs. Donovan?" Dr. Wells is used to repeating himself. Then he continues, "This isn't about batteries. It's the wrong make and model — older, underpowered. They look like yours, but they are not yours."

"Look, the serial number doesn't match the ones we issued to you at all. Where did you get these?"

"Uh, Lumira was the last one to handle my devices."

"Well, don't worry, Mrs. Donovan, we keep replacements here for emergencies. gesturing to the display cabinet. He continues, "If you've got ten minutes, I'll fit you with a proper set right now."

Grandma and Jane exchange a look — relief mixed with the realization that someone has tampered with her life in a very personal way.

"I can throw these old ones away for you."

"Oh, no," Jane says, "we will keep those too."

"You won't get them mixed up with the real ones?"

"No, Doctor. I won't."

Grandma walks out hearing the world clearly again. The game has quietly shifted in her favor. In the car Jane says, "Pearl, I hate to say it, but Lumira is up to something, and I feel it is something dangerous."

"Oh?" said Pearl, "she wants to fool around and find out?"

The two women laughed. Then Jane said, "I'm going to the bank now to open a safety deposit box, I think you should do the same and move some of your more sensitive documents and items out of reach of people who want to *fool around and find out.*"

"Now Pearl, hang on to those underpowered, underprivileged, subprime hearing aids that Lumira slipped you. And be sure every time she comes over you have these fake ones in. I can keep your real ones at my house on her visit days if you like. You do not need her to know that you are onto her."

Grandma's eyes open to the truth — she realizes her own daughter is dangerous. Grandma and Jane were developing a plan, and it was going to be epic.

At the bank she and Pearl open safety deposit boxes side by side. Grandma already has a box at this bank, but opens a second one that day with Jane, especially to put in things for Emily and keep them away from Lumira. Pearl only needs one key for this one. She begins quietly moving valuables into her safety deposit box. She put in deeds, bonds, a note for Emily — starting the chain of events that will one day expose the fake *family unit*: Lumira, Robert, and Melvin.

After those errands, Grandma Pearl Donovan stepped confidently into her house and walked up to that ugly bird and declared, "I don't know what you think you came here to do, but Back to Sender." Then Grandma took a pillowcase and covered it over. She would humor Lumira and uncover it on her visit days, but she was not going to be looking at that thing. Most of all, that thing was not going to be looking at her either.

Like A Sister

It's two years after that ugly bird carving, and the hearing aid incident. And it is one night since Jasmine told Emily that her Grandma had died.

The next morning at 6am, Jasmine was on a flight to Charlottesville, to Emily. She found her at the coffee shop. Jasmine was a sight for Emily's sore eyes that were puffy and red; she had been crying all night over her Grandma especially. But she'd also been lamenting that mother of hers and those people who she had believed were family.

Emily had not seen a relative for four semesters of college and two summers of two and three jobs. Worse, they were shunning her and didn't even want her to come home. Nothing was stopping them from coming to campus to see her but they didn't do that either, not even on parents' weekends.

As soon as she saw Jasmine, the waterworks started again, and she cried and cried as if there were any tears left in her.

Mrs. Richardson met Jasmine, and they were more than cordial, but bonded right away—like family that you've never met before. She then told Emily, "Go visit with your cousin. We'll be fine here. We'll see you back on Monday? Okay?"

"Yes, ma'am, thank you so much.

At Emily's room, Jasmine pulled up Grandma's obit and even her homegoing service was streamed. The whole family was there, but not Emily.

She showed Jasmine the texts from Grandma. She told her Grandma had sent her money every now and again.

"How are you surviving? Girl, I've been that broke student before myself. I've got some money. I can give it to you. I know you will pay me back when you graduate."

Emily pointed to Grandma's recipe box. "This is how I've been surviving."

"Cookies?"

"Yes, in a sense. That's how I've been surviving. Grandma gave me this box of recipe cards when I left for college and she said, 'One day these cookies will mean a lot to you.'"

"Okay--?"

"So that day, I was a little down, I took out the recipe box to bake. The box fell on the floor, and I found that Grandma had hidden cash money in it."

"Oh wow! Go Grandma!" Jasmine said.

They put their heads together to try to make sense of something that made no sense. Emily showed Jazz her texts thread with Grandma.

"Emm, what I'm noticing is that in two years of texting you, Grandma never asked you when you were coming home."

With a puzzled frown on her face, Emm gently took the phone from Jasmine. "OMG, you're right." She scrolled and then said, "She never said, I miss you or asked when I would be coming home."

"Emily, Grandma that's not like Grandma at all. Plus, Grandma is a class act; she would have sent you a ticket or money for a ticket."

"You are so right. I hadn't seen this." Emily stated clearly, "My family was pretending to be her. They were keeping up a fake act. For some reason they wanted me to believe that Grandma is still alive, but at the same time keeping me from coming back home because then I'd definitely find out."

"And why?"

"It wasn't because they loved me and wanted to shield me from the emotional pain. They are not like that."

"Then--,"

"Money," they both said together.

"Isn't it always about money?"

"Jasmine, Grandma was a retired, well-off businesswoman. My mother was always trying to get money from her, by hook or crook, but Grandma had stopped falling for her schemes and fake emergencies."

"So?"

"When Grandma died, my mother finally got her greedy little fingers on all that inheritance. That has got to be the answer."

"They said it was like 4 million dollars!" Jasmine asserted.

"Four million dollars! Emily gasped in disbelief.

"It could have been more."

"You mean, they are living it up – especially golden boy, Melvin?. And what did I get? Not that it is about money for me, but I know Grandma wouldn't leave me out."

"Jazz, Grandma was in my corner when I didn't even know I had a corner, or that there was a fight going on, or a boxing ring."

"And you girl—you are the best cousin in America – no, in the entire world. You are more like a real sibling to me than anyone. Thank you so much for coming up to see me. This means everything to me."

They sat in silence for a beat, then Emily continued, "They have been gaslighting me for years. I can't believe Grandma is gone."

Jasmine asked, "What are you going to do now?"

Without realizing it, Emily went to her dresser and picked up the recipe box again, ready to tell Jasmine about Miss Pearl's Cookies, but the box slipped from her nervous hands, and it fell again.

She was about to burst into tears when Jasmine screamed her cousin's name, "Emily!" This shocked Emily back to reality. "What is that key to?"

"What key?"

When the box fell a little compartment opened up and a key fell out.

"I don't know, Jazz, but we've got to go find out a lot of stuff and we can research this key too. I'm going back with you. We can leave in the morning. I'll ask Mrs. Richardson for the week off. She's really understanding, and this is an emergency."

Together Jasmine went with Emily to Grandma's house. It had been sold, so really, they went next door to Jane Womack's house.

Judge Jane Womack

Mrs. Womack was shocked to see Emily. "Emily, where have you been? They said no one knew where you were. Said you'd left home suddenly and left no forwarding address or phone number. They said you said you were disowning the family, they couldn't find you and you left a note that you didn't want to be found, and you wanted nothing from any family member whatsoever."

"*Whatsoever*—I don't talk like that. I went to college. I was at college. At UVA. I never wrote such a note, and everyone knew where I was."

"That's where I thought you were, but your family said they couldn't reach you, that you had dropped out of college and just left."

"That's not true, I'd never drop out of college; I'm on the Dean's list. School is too important to me."

"Of course, Emily. Because of that letter, they read the will without you. And dispersed the funds. Your mother being Pearl's only child--. They got their own lawyers, not listening to your Grandma Pearls lawyer, they said that you had forfeited any claim to any inheritance. So, they put it all in her hands, nearly 5 million dollars after they sold your grandmother's house next door. Your grandmother was quite a businesswoman."

"The will?"

"Yes, your grandma left you everything. She told me many times before that she didn't trust those vipers--, excuse me for talking about your relatives--,

"Miss Jane, Grandma ain't never lied about them—"

"--but Pearl said that you were the only genuine and honest one among them."

"Miss Jane – what do I do now?"

"Where are you staying?"

"She can stay with me," Jasmine said.

"Does your family know you're in town?"

"No,."

Then Judge Jane said, "I think Emily should stay here. You both can; I've got plenty of room. Monday morning, Emily, you are going with me to your Grandma's lawyer's office. Her lawyer –Ratcliffe --that boy – well he's old now but he clerked for me when I was a judge. We will get this sorted out."

"Isn't it too late, they already got Grandma's inheritance and they've been spending like crazy from what I hear?" She looks at Jasmine, who nods, for confirmation.

"Emily, it is never too late for justice – trust me. I was a judge for 30 years."

"Miss Jane? Emily realizes that what she called her mom's best friend when she was a kid, but she's not a kid anymore. Respect is due. I mean, "Judge Jane?"

"Yes dear."

"I have one more question – well me and Jasmine found this key. Do you have any idea what it is to? We can't go into Grandma's house anymore since it's been sold. I guess my mother sold it, right?"

"Yes, only a month after the funeral."

Judge Jane, we don't have any clues about this key."

"That, my dear Emily, is the key to a safety deposit box. First Bank & Trust. I know because I took your grandma there many times when she didn't feel like driving."

"And I also know because I have a similar key. I also know her box number because we opened our bank security boxes on the same day and requested, they be side by side."

"I guess my family has been all through it?"

"No ma'am, not without that key. Not only that, I have all the papers regarding that safe deposit box, Pearl insisted that I keep them here for you. They know nothing of that box."

"She left that for me?" queried Emily.

"Yes, Emily. Looks like Pearl had more tricks up her sleeve than we knew. I do happen to know that she had some valuable and sentimental things in that bank box."

"Will you take me there?"

"Yes, Emily, I will."

The Trove at First Bank & Trust

Inside the safe deposit vault, Emily inserted the key and the drawer opened. She found nice jewelry, even Grandma Pearl's pearl necklace. She put it on. she used to wear some of these pieces when she played dress up as a kid. She had no idea they were real and expensive.

As she sorted through everything, she found another key. This one had a number etched on it. Grandma had a second safe deposit box.

With the help of the banker, Emily opened that one. In it were old papers – deeds.

Financial & Legal documents included:

Original copy of Grandma's will, signed and fully notarized, naming Emily as the sole heir.

Old savings bonds and **certificates of deposit**; worth a lot.

A small ledger notebook tracking every dollar the family took… and what they owe.

A **gold locket** with a photo of young Emily on one side, and Grandma on the other.

A wedding ring (possibly not Grandma's, but her mother's, in a small envelope with a note, *"You are the future of this family. Don't let them dim your light or silence your voice."*

A recipe card — The first cookie recipe they ever made together — with a faded cocoa stain and handwriting that says, *"This one always made you smile."*

A small journal with personal notes, stories, and words of advice just for Emily

Photographs of Emily and Grandma baking, laughing, learning together — tucked in a little envelope marked *"my favorite memories."* Emily remembered Jane taking those photos back in the day. Jane was really like an aunt to her.

Grandma was smart, low-key strategic, and not playing about her legacy. She had properties scattered across neighborhoods, many in vibrant, bustling Chicago, not the small town where she lived in Indiana. Grandma even had some commercial spaces, and held onto them quietly for decades.

The family knew Grandma had money but had no idea how much. So, when they liquidated what they thought was her estate they thought that was it. They thought that was all and they were all grins and began to party and waste instead of being sober and continuing to build on what Grandma had built.

All totaled, Grandma had more than 40 million in real estate assets. She was quietly wealthy, and she kept her real wealth from the vipers. She had more than a dozen rental properties in Chicago. She owned small commercial buildings. As Emily would research and find out later, she'd find that there were viable businesses occupying these buildings. A storefront, a laundromat, a barbershop, and all these businesses were making their lease payments.

Grandma had land plots she inherited or invested in. She even owned one historic property that's now worth a fortune. Emily's heart was racing at the sheer business savvy, intelligence and foresight of her Grandma.

She found another deed to an apartment complex that Grandma had bought back when it was undervalued, but at today's market value the apartment complex alone is worth more than 12 million and every square foot belongs to Emily.

Emily didn't just inherit a fortune, she inherited an empire. built on Grandma's vision, protected by love, and now in the hands of someone who'll honor it and continue to build and add to it.

Emily's inherited real estate portfolio valued at: $42.7 million. Residential Properties ($17M). Six duplexes on Chicago's south side, all income-producing, fully rented.

3 brownstones in up-and-coming neighborhoods — classic architecture, high value.

2 lakefront homes (one rented, one a future retreat)

1 office building rented by small Black-owned businesses (Grandma was intentional)

Vacant Land ($4.5M). 4 city lots quietly increasing in value that Grandma had owned for 30+ years.

1 inherited parcel in Mississippi, where Grandma's parents were from. It was rural, but possibly there might be oil/mineral rights to be leased or sold.

A warehouse near the train line — currently vacant, full of potential

An empty lot across from a school — zoning hints at future development

And one last thing in the folder: a handwritten note:

> *"Don't sell it all. Build something they can't take from you. Love, Grandma."*

Emily whispered to herself, My Grandma was a visionary, a business genius. She shook her head at the thought that Lumira was nothing like her own mother. Nothing at all. Had she learned nothing from Grandma, or was she just not capable of learning? All Lumira wanted to do was party and spend, spend and party. While Grandma built and saved.

More reality hit Emily as she could clearly see that now she has: monthly rental income as well as the lump sum of all that had been collected in the past two years since Grandma had passed. The property management company didn't often hear from Grandma anyway, they just managed all the properties, collected the rents, and directly deposited her rents and proceeds in yet another bank under her trust and holding funds which the family had absolutely no knowledge of. (Go Grandma!)

Weeks before her transition, Grandma must have realized that she was having clear days and foggy days. On one of her clear days, she had changed her mailing address for every document to the management company. When Emily met them, they gave her all the cards and letters she had written to Grandma. Emily thought to herself, after she realized when Grandma had transitioned, *no wonder they hadn't been returned to her in the mail.* This was a bittersweet moment, the memory of Grandma, but the lost connection and she hadn't even known it.

Young, but wise, when she would meet with them, Emily put her business face back on and continued with the meeting.

She learned that the management company had sent all quarterly and annual statements and documents to Pearl Donovan's designated CPA firm. Emily would continue with that same firm.

Emily had equity to leverage. She had property to develop. She had a seat at the table and the keys to the building—all the buildings. Seemed her parents kept her broke so she wouldn't come home and find out that Grandma had passed. They never knew how tight Emily and Jasmine were, that they talked regularly and that Jasmine would be instrumental in Emily finding out the truth.

Grandma was old-school. Smart. Private. In the second safety security box, Emily found a thick envelope that read: Negotiable Instrument — Bearer Bond Enclosed. Bearer Bonds were phased out in the late 1990s, but Grandma's were still valid because they were issued before the cutoff and never redeemed. Inside were $500,000 in old bearer bonds, tucked in an envelope marked, *Just In Case*. She left them in the envelope but flipped through them just enough to see what they were then pushed them back in to the envelope for another time. They were unregistered; only Emily has access now. Absolutely legal to claim and redeem (after verification by the bank and the IRS. Emily decided she'd deal with these bearer bonds, but later.

Emily isn't just inheriting money, she's uncovering secrets, strategy, and power that Grandma protected in silence.

Emily found out about a lot of what these documents meant at Grandma's lawyer's office. Attorney Ratcliffe was shocked to see me, but quickly said, "If they knew where you were the whole time, then what they did wasn't just cold. It was illegal. They'd committed inheritance theft. Fraud."

Attorney Ratcliffe began helping Emily sort out all she found in the safe deposit boxes. He personally took her to her Grandmother's financial planner and they all worked together to transfer some things into her name, but most things were left into the holding company Pearl Legacy Group and Emily took over it.

Emily said to herself, "I wasn't about to let them get away with stealing from me... or from Grandma. Not these greedy Santorini, globetrotting vultures."

Turns out, everything they did — faking texts, hiding Grandma's death, blowing through my inheritance — was straight-up fraud. They thought I'd just stay quiet and struggle in college while they lived it up on my money? Yeah... no.

That summer I was home alright but I wasn't at my family's house – wherever they lived now. I filed charges. Took them to court. And trust me... the judge did not go easy on them.

Not because of selfishness or greed, but to honor Grandma's legacy, and put some respect on Grandma's name, Emily took those happy evil thieves to court.

Emily kept the real inheritance to herself. If these vultures ever found out what Grandma was really sitting on they may freak out. What weren't they willing to do? Emily got a cold chill up her spine as she wondered, was she even safe around these money grubbers?

After their shock that Emily was home – they looked around as to ask, how did she get here? How did she get money to get a lawyer and file these papers? What they didn't know is that Grandma had prepaid Mr. Ratcliffe a huge retainer for Emily's sake. It had been just sitting in escrow for such a time as this. Grandma had said to Ratcliffe one day when she came by and handed him a check for $50,000, saying, "This is for future use. My granddaughter, Emily will contact you at the appropriate time."

In court the fake family unit's defense was weak and shameless. My lawyer called them out. Full-on called them liars, fraudsters, thieves. It was like watching bad actors in a cheap play. They stuttered, sputtered, murmured and complained. Said they 'didn't want to upset me' while I was away at school. Said it was 'for my own good.'"

That's not what the forfeiture letter said, as Grandma's lawyer, now my lawyer entered that into evidence.

My own mother and father hit me with every manipulation tactic in the book — *'You misunderstood.' 'We thought it was best.' 'We're a family, we share.'"*

Funny thing is... my brother was blowing through that inheritance money like it's nothing. And me? Now that I've got real working capital, once I finish Darden and get my degree, I'll be out here like Grandma, building a life they can't touch.

In court, my attorney cited Inheritance Theft. Misappropriation of Funds. Forgery. Impersonation. These people were outrageous. Not only did they pretend to be Grandma — sending texts, making it seem like she was alive, my own mother had hired an actress who looked somewhat like me who would pretend to be me if the fake letter that said I didn't want any inheritance didn't work. They had even prepared a fake ID for this actress. That letter got them the inheritance instead of me.

The actress? Well, Melvin had tried to date her and treated her so badly that when she found out about the stolen inheritance, she realized that it wasn't an acting role, but it was criminal. She had called Mr. Ratcliffe's office and issued an affidavit that the Judge accepted.

Eww, why would Melvin try to date someone who looked like me – his own sister? These people are creepy.

They were also charged with Failure to Notify Next of kin. Estate Fraud for illegally dividing Grandma's estate, ignoring her will, and keeping my rightful inheritance. We had to file a separate claim for that in Probate Court. The filings were comprehensive: Inheritance theft, conversion, fraud.

I stayed silent and got my Justice the right way, the legal way, the quiet way. I went full force.

They had to pay back every dollar they stole, with interest. And legal fees. And the best part? The court made it a public record, so everyone knew exactly who they were and what they did. Lumira, Robert and Melvin all now have records although they got probation.

After that? I was done. Done with them. These people were not my family. Family doesn't behave like this.

Two years later I graduated from college. I wasn't sure if I wanted to continue to get an MBA, but I was already in business with Miss Pearl's Cookies and working with my surrogate mom, Mrs. Richardson. It was refreshing and joyful.

So, I changed my name. Moved away from these vipers. I continued in business and kept my vow to make Grandma proud. They tried reaching out — apologizing, begging, even trying to play the 'we're family' card. I left them on read.

They took everything, including Grandma. But in the end? I took everything back... and walked away with something they'll never have: peace. Some people think family is forever... but betrayal is a choice. And walking away from the vipers as Grandma had called them--, that was mine.

Lumira

They thought they could get away with it but no! This wasn't some petty little inheritance. My grandma was wealthy. I knew our family wasn't poor. I am astounded at how naïve I had been to worry that they were suffering when they hadn't sent me any money for college. I inherited nearly 50 million in cash, investments, and real estate.

What Grandma had set out in plain sight, they didn't just take it… they blew through it like it was pocket change. Cars. Vacations, I found out when the texts would slow down, when they were on vacation because they didn't take Grandma's phone with them. Plus, they were afraid that it would have a location stamp if they sent me anything from it while abroad. While they were on holiday, they forgot all about me and probably Grandma, too, but they kept her phone service active.

They spent so much money doting on my brother. All while I was struggling just to pay rent and eat, living like an orphan.

Thank God for Mrs. Richardson who was like a mother to me.

Anyway, those blood relatives, I hit them where it hurt the most — in court. And when the truth came out, they didn't just have to pay me back every dollar — the judge hit them with damages, legal fees, and penalties.

They had to liquidate everything they had bought with that stolen money, including the new McMansion that Lumira had insisted on buying, which My attorney and Judge Jane had no problem locating the address.

The sale of Grandma's house had to be unraveled, reversed and undone. The people who had bought the house from Lumira and Robert turned around and sued them too. Let's just say… they lost a whole lot more than they stole.

Once the case was over, Emm and Jasmine hugged like real sisters. Emily went on to change her last name to her Grandmother's surname, Donovan, and hyphenated it with Richardson because Mrs. Richardson became more like a mother to her than her real mother.

I asked Mrs. Richardson to adopt me because I had already adopted her as my mother.

Some of what I would have shared with my family if they hadn't treated me so badly, I gave to Jasmine to get her off to a good start in life. My Cousin-sister, Jasmine, is now a millionaire too because real family shares.

I taught Jazz how to be a quiet businesswoman, so leeches won't always be trying to hit you up for money. But Jasmine has a special gift of making people comfortable enough to talk and never letting them know that she's gathering information. Then she has the skill of keeping her mouth shut when it needs to be shut. She's opened her first business. Along with Judge Jane they started an online detective agency. It's a national company; She does a lot of research online then she hires local private investigators to do the footwork and get pictures and videos. It is quite successful. Next, she is looking into real estate. Go Jazz!

I disappeared. Well, I didn't really disappear, I silently run and invest in businesses that make me even more successful than Grandma was – guess I got her genes for money making after all. They had no idea how successful I had become. I didn't even do it to show them. I did it for me; to show myself that I am not only enough, some days, I am so tough that I might be more than enough. I did it for Grandma to protect all she had worked for in a lifetime. So yeah… sometimes the people you think are in your corner are the ones holding the knife. Just because they share your blood doesn't mean they won't try to draw it. It doesn't mean that they'll ever have your back.

They tried to reach out. Tried to '*make peace.*' Nope. You don't steal from me, lie to me, make me suffer for years, all alone--, and then act like nothing happened. I have so many staff and security people around me now, they couldn't get to me even if they knew where I lived. Of course I travel a lot for work, so they can't keep up with me.

The Legacy

Emily knew exactly how to celebrate and honor Grandma's legacy.

Painful and emotional lessons learned: in addition to the cookies – Miss Pearl's Cookies, Emily knew exactly what to do next and how to honor her grandma's legacy.

Emily presented a business plan to Mrs. Richardson that on every campus where there was a future Richardson's Coffee they would build a new building for the coffee shop that would be on the first floor of an apartment building for smart students, whether they won scholarships or not, but those who really could not afford housing. Eight doubles with ensuites, very nice units where a student could be safe and comfortable and also live with dignity while they attended college. And, they would also do a work study program by working in the coffee shop.

Emily, that is genius, that is 16 workers for each coffee shop.

Yes, it will be like family, but with dignity and they wouldn't have to worry about housing while they get their education. If we don't get enough lower income students, we can rent at market rates to regular students because these apartment suites will be nice.

And, for business majors who show promise while working in the coffee shop, we can offer them a franchise, with financing, and they can continue running the coffee shop as their own.

Emily, this is an excellent plan. How will we finance this?

Momma Richardson, my Grandmother left a legacy and I have to give back to others who have promise but who may not have means. We will pay this forward, but you will get a nice payday for every franchise that you sell.

The two shook hands like two real business partners. Then they hugged like mother to daughter.

It was exhilarating, the building the developing, creating the foundation that would make room for students seeking to better their lives even though they may not have had the support that they needed or deserved. They saw the vision the same and they worked together very well. So far, they have built three apartment units with the downstairs coffee shops. They had started in Virginia since there was already one at UVA. They built one at ODU, William & Mary, and VCU. The University of Richmond was next as soon as they could procure the land in a viable spot for the coffee shop and housing. Instead of building, they had taken over and renovated a small boutique style hotel in Fredericksburg for Mary Washington students. Coffee and Cookies were a hit everywhere.

As much of a job of joy for Mrs. Richardson, she loved the franchise paydays and the release of the responsibility to oversee the coffee shops as her regional managers reported to her. This would free her up to build another one. She was hooked.

Emily was hooked too, but she was obeying the wishes of Grandma Pearl, '*Build something that they can't take away from you.*' The franchisees of the coffee shops would still pay rent and Emily & Mrs. Richardson would still co-own the buildings. The students paid some rent, based on a sliding scale.

Never Too Late for Justice

Some days it still makes me sad that they took everything — including Grandma. Grandma was the real deal, and I didn't even get to say goodbye to her. But in the end... I took my life back. And they'll be stuck with their shame, their debt, and each other.

Me? I'm living the life Grandma wanted for me. On my terms. And far, far away from the vipers. Oh, I'm sure they have enough, my father is still working incessantly to repay all they stole and also so my mother can continue spoiling Melvin.

But after court, Lumira burst out why she did it: she was always jealous of my relationship with her mother and was afraid that Grandma would leave me inheritance and not her. Well, that was exactly what happened. Man, my mother had issues! However, this is not my problem and not my concern anymore.

It's a shame when people you are related to are toxic and should be avoided.

So yeah... I learned the hard way. Family doesn't always mean loyalty. Sometimes, they'll look you in the face and lie while you're barely surviving.

Taped to the Back

Grandma was old school with the bearer bonds, but she was up to date in other ways. She even had Bitcoin; I found her layered log in credentials and password to Coinbase in the other safe deposit box.

Emily had brought all the documents out of the safe deposit box. She would keep them in the safe in her penthouse and open another deposit box in a closer bank. One day she pulled the envelope out that she had kept until last. She looked at the old school deeds and deep in the envelope with the Bearer Bonds she saw a small note written on pink paper in her grandmother's distinctive handwriting. She hadn't seen that before.

On the back of a Bearer bond document that Emily had looked at surely over the months since she opened the safe deposit box she found taped to the back of one of the Bearer Bonds, this cryptic note:

'Dear Emily: If you see this in time, as soon as you left for college, I believe Lumira started switching my medication. Every time she comes over, I feel different, weaker. If anything happens to me, don't let her get away with it. Grandma.'

Emily placed her hand over her heart and gasped suddenly. She was in a daze, but only for a few moments. She picked up the phone and dialed Judge Jane Womack. "Judge, I have found a most damning note, is there any statute of limitations on murder?"

"No, Emily, it is never too late for justice. I was wondering when you'd call me about this because I had my suspicions all along."

Three hours later Emily and Jasmine stood talking to Judge Jane's video doorbell. She was dressed and ready to go. They were disappointed, "We didn't know you had someplace to go, we wanted to talk to you about this---," Emily waved Grandma's note.

"Ladies," Judge Jane said, "I'm driving, jump in the car, we are going somewhere."

Jane pulled up to a gorgeous villa on the Northshore. Emily squinted but then she recognized the address; it matched one of the deeds in the second safety deposit box.

"Wow, this is beautiful" Jasmine wanted to know, of Judge Jane, "Is this your villa?"

"No, mine is next door. We are visiting a good friend of mine today."

This particular address belonged to Grandma.

"I thought so," whispered Emily, so engrossed and looking around.

They walked up to the front door, and it opened for them. A person in a maid's outfit opened the door. Inside a lovely brunch table was set with nice China and crystal glasses.

They smelled wonderful smells from the nearby kitchen; it smelled like all of Emily's favorite foods: Italian.

"Oh, it's a party."

"No, it's a reunion."

"Oh, I didn't see any other cars in the driveway---"

Emily stopped cold in her tracks. There stood Grandma. She wanted to run to her, but she didn't even know if she was real, if this place was real, if she was dreaming, she just didn't know.

Jasmine was just as bad; confused. They were both sobbing.

"Emily, my dear Emily. My little bunny."

Oh, that was Grandma, no one else dared call her Bunny. "Grandma, you're, you're-."

"Yes I am."

"Why are you here? How are you here? What's going on, Grandma?"

"Sit down and I'll tell you all about it."

Emily first had to get control of her ugly crying face. She freshened up in the powder room then they all sat down for a nice meal and heavy conversation.

Taking Care of Grandma

After dinner and each staring at a piece of tiramisu and fresh coffee, Jasmine said, "Emm, I was looking online, and I hadn't seen these pictures before of your family in Mumbai."

"Mumbai?"

"Oh yeah, Lumira brought me a souvenir from that trip."

"What was it?"

"Well, it was more than one thing, but it was this ugly eyesore she hung on the wall." Jane had a picture of it on her cell phone and started showing it to the girls. "She brought me whatever she was putting in my tea, I suspect sleeping pills she ground into a powder, and she may have gotten the idea to switch my meds from whoever advised her in her travels."

Jane testified, "I saw her, I have video of her tampering *with or adding something to Pearl*'s tea. I had placed an undercover camera in the kitchen."

"Lumira took my checkbook telling me she would pay my bills, but I checked my balance daily; they drained that account. I only let them do it to make them think they were winning, and I wanted to see how low they would go".

"They went pretty low, Grandma."

"Yes, they did, Bunny. But the worst thing they did was to keep you and I apart, to keep us from communicating." Both Grandma and Emily had tears streaming again at the same time they were smiling because they were together. It was like a rainstorm while the sun is also shining. What you see probably depends on who you are. Do you see the rain, or do you see the sun?

Grandma's own daughter, Lumira, went several times a week to "check on" Grandma but she switched Grandma's medication, every time she went, giving her own mother some fake sugar pill or other non-medication.

"She was putting sleep medicine or some sedative in your tea Pearl. Every time I came over after her visits it's like you were zonked out."

"Well, at first. Soon I began to just act like I had drank the tea and pretended to get groggy, just to get her to leave, already."

Pearl and Jane chuckled a guarded laugh and Pearl said, "Near about turned me and Jane into pharmacists, we counted pills every week. We had whatever Lumira was giving me – it was candy. I was sure to take my real medication before the day ended."

"Emily, I wanted you to have everything, especially after I learned those three, the unit is what I've named them were trying to kill me."

"Grandma!"

"They don't know a thing about this house where we are now, so I came here for my own safety. And I had always thought I'd retire here anyway. So, with Jane's help, I fake died in my sleep. I had a fake death certificate made."

Jane said, "We called in a lot of favors. I got some fake ashes put into an urn, but we had a real mortician pretend that was Pearl and held a memorial service. No casket, just cremains."

Grandma then said, "I had written a note that I wanted immediate cremation and a simple service. Yeah, we had our own fake letters.

"Lumira and the unit were happy about the fast cremation because they thought it would help cover their crimes.

"We found out about the pill swap when Jane took me to the doctor a couple of times when I was feeling weak, once to Urgent Care but another time to my regular doctor.

Jane noticed a discrepancy in the pharmacy records — dates and meds don't match prescriptions.

Why do you have pills left over at the end of the month, Mrs. Donovan? Aren't you taking your meds?" is what they always wanted to know at the doctor's offices."

"Yes," I told them, 'Every day.' But for the first month you were gone I had the same number of prescription pills left over matching how many days Lumira came over to help me and administer my medication to me, 14. I didn't need her doing that, I've been taking my own meds by myself for years but she insisted I take the meds in front of her—the fake sugar pills she had brought over in a real prescription bottle that she had stolen from me. She came over 14 times in that month, making sure I saw her take the fake pill out of the bottle. It was quite a performance. But, she hadn't thought it all the way through; I had 14 more real pills than I should have at the end of the month.

"Jane thinks she saw Lumira taking bottles in and out every visit – Jane has video. She had her house cameras trained on Pearl's house and her video doorbell captured some odd things.

Jane says, "Pearl authorized me to access her medical records so we could look at these things together. It was glaring."

Emily was hearing this truth for the first time — her face in frozen disbelief, Jasmine looking ready to fight, Jane calmly sliding a file folder and thumb drives across the table with the evidence inside.

Lumira's sinister routine went something like this: She arrives all smiles — but Jane notices Grandma's energy changes *after* she leaves. She brings a "care bag" every time — inside are pill bottles as if she stopped at the Pharmacy for her mother. Fresh batteries for Grandma's hearing aid since Grandma didn't hear well. Sometimes she would bring fresh fruit and other groceries, but not every visit.

Jane would come promptly over and throw away everything she brought into the house.

While there, Lumira does weird things. She lingers by the tea or coffee pot, using it as an opportunity for slipping a light powder into Grandma's tea. She fake changes the batteries in Grandma's hearing aids, but really, she switches her mother's hearing device for a wrong or broken set.

"Is that why I couldn't talk to you all those years, fake hearing aids?"

"Oh, we were onto her the first time Bunny, but I missed you so much but had to make this authentic. I'm sorry I didn't reach out to you all this time, but it was a matter of life and death, really."

One day in June or July, on her way out Lumira takes Grandma's checkbook, tells her it's just to pay the bills at her brownstone, although she knows she will use as much money as she can get out of that account.

"Oh yeah, I remember I was still seated at the table, sipping tea, a little tired and she said, *"I'll just take care of those bills for you, Mama." What she meant was she was taking my checkbook.'"*

As Lumira left that day, Jane was watching through the window as Lumira leaves with that checkbook, planting the seed of suspicion.

Lumira? She's the kind of villain who smiles while twisting the knife. For the past 18 years she has lived in Emily's shadow, mumbling to herself for years, "Grandma thinks more of Emily than me. Well, Mama, Emily is gone now – it's just me and you."

Lumira is switching real meds out for candy so Grandma is not getting her proper dosages. In addition, she is putting sleeping pill powder or maybe even a sedative in her own mother's tea, mixed with Lord knows what else.

Jane's sharp eye picked up that Grandma is *always more tired* after Lumira's visits--, it's not like they went hiking so she shouldn't be that tired. Jane secretly gifts Pearl a phone charger that has a hidden camera in it and puts it in the kitchen by the coffee machine and tea kettle. She just wants to know that Pearl is taking her medications, and she is, regularly. Jane connects it to her own phone instead of Pearl's so Lumira won't find out that it's not just a phone charger.

I saw it on camera, Lumira opens a small packet in her hand, discreetly shaking a fine powder into Grandma's cup of tea while chatting casually. She stirs slowly, keeping eye contact with Grandma, making it seem like normal care. She keeps stirring until she can no longer see the faint swirl of powder in her own mother's tea.

Grandma says, "'Lumira, I said to her one time, You know I prefer coffee; I don't want this, you drink it.' But she said back to me, 'No, Ma, tea is more therapeutic, it's healthier for you. So, you drink it.' Lumira insists. So, when she wouldn't drink it, I wouldn't touch it.

"I had a tantrum and told her I wanted coffee. She didn't have any more powder. So, I forced her to pour that out and make me coffee that day."

Everyone at the dinner party burst out laughing.

Grandma's health would appear to "decline naturally" — she's drowsy, forgetful, weak. Lumira gets to play the *devoted daughter*, visiting often and "helping" while actually hastening her decline.

"Pearl you became a great actress in those weeks, didn't you?" Grandma and Jane slap high fives at the table.

Two months after Emily no longer visited, Grandma goes to sleep and that's it. It's sudden, and it is a part of their epic plan.

Lumira is not acting alone, both Robert and Melvin know that Grandma is declining--, albeit a forced decline, but they don't come to visit her or see about her; they don't care as long as their own lives are going as they want.

They are all three greedy, and selfish, but Lumira is sociopathic toward her own mother; Lumira is homicidally jealous and greedy.

Robert helps drain Grandma's bank accounts. He practiced forging Grandma's signature. He moves the money from Grandma's accounts to offshore modalities to cover Lumira's tracks so she won't brazenly steal everything while Grandma is still alive. And, how could she describe where she got the money to the IRS, so she couldn't pay taxes on it. This is a full family conspiracy, where *everyone in that household* benefits from Grandma's death. Grandma was right; these are vipers.

Grandma intended for Emily to inherit *everything*, which would leave the son with nothing. Lumira found this out because Grandma planted a fake will for Lumira to find. That Will indicated the only real estate Grandma owned was her brownstone she lived in, along with some cash accounts. Lumira, no only worships Melvin but she also thinks she deserves to live large on the money she thinks her mother has by work, investments and inheritance. Lumira's father who died young, running in the streets with the wrong crowd getting his "hustle on" left a life insurance policy and Lumira has always believed that it was for her and her alone.

"Wow, you were onto them," says Jasmine.

"Oh, baby, you can't fool and old *fooler,*" says Grandma.

The group laughed and then Jane continued.

"Robert would often meet Lumira at Grandma's house after her *visits,* but he never goes in. They drive off in separate cars, just the way they came. Lumira usually hands him something, like a large envelope."

"After your fake death, Miss Pearl, Melvin suddenly has expensive new things all the time."

Lumira had no intention of tampering with the Will, but she had other ideas that would net her the inheritance and not Emily.

Jasmine concludes, "So Lumira, Uncle Robert, and Melvin all went to Mumbai and there met a spiritualist who told them what to do to accomplish this evil, and he performed some witchcraft rituals for a large sum of money. The witchcraft guy told them, that it was so they wouldn't get caught. That trip was a secret, but I've figured this much out because my cousin, Melvin, was bragging."

Mumbai

When Lumira took Grandma's checkbook that day, Grandma had 98 thousand and some change in that checking account. The first thing Lumira did was to write herself a check to withdraw half of it. That felt good. Liberating. Intoxicating. Powerful.

She liked having access to thousands of dollars and she knew her mother had more, but she needed to devise a new way to get it because all of her other tactics had stopped working on her mother.

She researched online and found out that people--, many people go to certain destinations to procure "help" in accomplishing difficult tasks. This kind of help would be secret and may be found on the back streets of certain countries known to have communities who specialized in this sort of thing. She would go for "spiritual" power to help her finally get her hands on her inheritance that she felt she deserved. Lumira knew that if she didn't, Emily would surely get the bulk of it if not all, and Lumira's mother was getting old.

She decided on Mumbai. Flights were cheap, hotels weren't bad. For travel and lodging, excursions, shopping, and dining she budgeted 25 to 30 thousand for the three of them. She had an overseas friend who knew a person who had a friend who provided certain services for a hefty price. They agreed to connect her. This planning started in June, before Emily ever went to college. This was planned long before Emily left the state.

Lumira, her husband, and her son travel under the guise of a "business opportunity" or "vacation," but it was actually to meet with a *spiritualist* in the back streets of Mumbai. She gave the spiritualist 20 thousand dollars. So Grandma's 98 thousand was now 48 thousand and her own money was being spent to hurt her. Lumira was heartless.

The spiritualist performs several **rituals** that promise that Grandma will die quickly but appear to have passed naturally. And that suspicion will fall on no one. And most important to Lumira, the path to controlling her wealth will be "cleared." This includes *instructions* for the med swap + tea tampering, plus symbolic items to hide in Grandma's home.

While they are there, Robert and Melvin act like they are at a mall of evil genies. Robert asks for business success and is given an elaborate carved walking stick. Melvin wants popularity with females, and he is given a golden bracelet to wear to make him irresistible to women. Those items were already prepared, seems like those are common requests. You'd think he would have asked to be drafted by the NBA, but this is Melvin. Go figure.

Robert is quiet about what Lumira's grand scheme is, but he is also complicit, enjoying the new stream of money.

Melvin is careless —, young and dumb. He buys flashy clothes, electronics, and lets little things slip. He brags to Jasmine in a moment of showing off) about "that trip" and hints they "came back with all the answers."

Online Detective

Jasmine knows because she does deep online research. Something inside of her won't let this go. She also knows because Melvin is a motor mouth and he keeps her interested by the things he says to her.

"Look at the time stamp on this Mumbai picture," Jasmine says to Emily. "This is four years ago, the week you left for university. The moment you left they took a trip. Looks like he held on to this one for a minute but now has decided to post it. Guess Melvin couldn't wait to post another vacation pic, for the *ladies*," she said sarcastically.

"Jasmine, you say *they*, but only Melvin is in any of these pictures."

"Emily, do you think Melvin is capable of international travel on his own even if he did have money?"

"Well, no."

"I know they all went because your Dad came to tell us they'd be gone for a week, where they were going and that everyone was going. So, they all went to Mumbai together."

Melvin is probably alone in the pictures – to look cool, most likely--, for the *ladies*. Who wants to be on trips with their parents if you're posting online?"

Judge Jane can confirm that, she says, "I can find out through connections at the State Department where their passports were stamped." Seems the *Unit* didn't realize that Grandma and Jane are best friends--, like sisters and they see each other every day. Jane said, "Your Grandma was fine that entire time. Her health didn't start getting wonky until after they got back from that overseas excursion."

Then one day, Melvin is over talking to Jasmine and lets slip about Mumbai while boasting about his "custom-made" shoes from

India. "Look" he said, "me and dad got matching shoes while we were there."

"Where?" I asked him. He just kept running his mouth and then said, "Mumbai."

"Emily, that got me digging."

"So what did they do there?

"Emm, you know your brother is not a genius, right? He also bragged about a charm that he got there so the ladies would love him."

"A charm, like a lucky rabbit's foot?"

"A charm, like witchcraft," interjects Jane.

"But his happens to be either a bracelet or on a bracelet," says Jasmine. "I know, I saw it."

"Oh," Emily gasped.

"That's why he kept posting pictures of himself so the ladies would see him and slide into his DM's."

"Motor mouth Melvin? I asked him if his charm was working on the ladies. He grinned devilishly and said, 'all the charms work, we all got one'."

"What does that mean, Melvin? I asked him."

"The ladies are sliding into my DM's, dad's business is thriving he is making more money than ever before. Nothing can stop us now."

I hesitated, but then asked anyway, "And your mom?"

That's when he shut up and looked away like a guilty fool.

Emily was devastated, "This wasn't just financial fraud; it was planned evil, planned harm."

Jane texted a picture to Jasmine's phone of the raven lotus carving. "Oh, I just got it -- Give me a minute, let me research that thing."

Jane starts up again, "That wooden raven sculpture, inlaid with tiny red gemstones for the eyes that seemed to watch. Carved with Hindi or Sanskrit symbols. I hated that thing; it gave me the creeps. When touched, it felt bone chilling cold and slimy, kind of oily. I'm from New Orleans and I know there was something dark about that thing."

Grandma spoke up, "Lumira had said, *'Just a little something to watch over you when I can't be here.'"*

"I always felt uneasy when I saw it. And Pearl didn't you start having strange dreams after it arrived?"

"Yes, one dream in particular that repeated, a dream of that bird talking and laughing. In one dream the bird was defecating in a cage, defecating small gold coins. It was so bizarre. It was unsettling, actually."

"Grandma, what did you do?"

"I got up that morning and prayed, Emily. I canceled the dream; it was a devil dream. Then I prayed that whatever that thing came to do I stop it in the Name of Jesus."

"Yes! Go, Grandma!" exclaimed both Emily and Jasmine.

"Grandma."

"Yes, Emily."

"I just noticed you are not wearing hearing aids."

"Oh, I got cochlear implants finally."

"Grandma, that's awesome, why hadn't you done that before?"

"Lumira always talked me out of it."

"I've had them for three years now and everything is solved. I can hear just fine."

"Grandma, I'm so glad," gushed Emily.

Right then, Jasmine connects the object to an image she finds in an article about "occult death rites" from Mumbai.

Grandma continues, "I left them enough money to entertain and entrap themselves – to make them feel like they had done something. I left them enough to distract them along with thinking I was gone so they wouldn't keep trying to poison or deprive me of medication and care. I left them enough to have money to send you Emily for your schooling."

"Oh Grandma, they didn't send me much at all."

"What! They didn't send you money for college?"

"Not exactly Grandma I got a few dollars here and there the first year, then I got $250 a month the second year."

"Two fifty a month, while they had millions? How did you make it, Emily?"

"I had to work."

"While in school?"

"Yes, Grandma. If it had not been for Mrs. Richardson—".

"Richardson? The coffee lady?"

"Yes."

"Bless her heart. Anyone who has helped you, I'd like to meet."

"Grandma, I'll make it happen. We have been doing some business together."

"Emily," Grandma continued, "Lumira and her unit are far worse than I thought. I'm glad then that the rest I put in a Living Trust for you Emily so you could inherit it—the real inheritance.

"I was so proud of Miss Pearl's Cookies."

"You knew about the cookies?"

"Yes. I kept up with you, Bunny. You're making money right now, aren't you?"

"Yes, I am."

"I just want to say," says Jane, "that Lumira didn't shed a tear when her own mother fake-died."

Everyone at the table looked at each other awkwardly and then everyone burst out laughing. Grandma, along with Jane outsmarted those greedy people. The *Unit, the viper unit* as Grandma called them.

Then the laughter stops, and they get sober and serious again. Emily is staring down at *Grandma's note* from the safety deposit box — hands trembling. Emily looks up, confused, eyes still glassy. "What she did to Grandma is heartless."

Jane asserts, "Attempted matricide."

Emily swallows hard, fighting back fresh tears.

Jane continues, "But sometimes..." she leans in, with a low voice, says, "Lumira— her name may mean something good, but, sometimes the brightest light blinds you. And the wrong kind of peace... is silence."

Emily stares at Jane, the words hitting her like a punch. Jasmine reaches for her hand.

"No more silence!" blurts out Emily. "Is it too late for justice for Grandma?"

"It's never too late for justice," says Jane. We may not be able to prove the evil in that creepy souvenir, other than to show evil intent. But we definitely can prove the rest of it, Emily. We've got receipts."

The Slow Turn

A year after Grandma's fake death that the viper unit didn't know was fake, as she walks by it to the kitchen to make coffee, Lumira's lotus-raven wall hanging seems to shift in the corner of her eye. No, this is not a copy of the one she gave her mother; it is the same one that she gave Grandma. After Grandma's demise she brought it home and hung it on her own wall. She was proud of what she had accomplished. But did this bird move? Was she imagining things? She had been having weird dreams that the bird was telling her that they needed to go back to Mumbai. *Huh?* She wasn't going back to that place. She had gotten what she wanted from there and there were many nicer places to visit. She thought Dubai would be the next trip. They had *arrived*; they were jetsetters now. She didn't have time to listen to a bird, obey a bird, or even argue with a bird. A bird! Ridiculous, she exclaimed.

The husband's "souvenir" a carved walking stick he thought, made him looked distinguished and important. But it starts turning up in unexpected places in the house. He leaves it in the bedroom; he finds it in the hallway. He leaves it in the hallway, it ends up in the kitchen or the garage. I know that is not where I left that walking stick, Lumira, he mumbles. Then he exclaims, "Has Melvin been moving my things?"

"No, Robert, Melvin wasn't even here. He went camping with some buddies yesterday."

"Lumira, can't you see him sitting right here on the couch with that Play Station thing?"

"Oh, Melvin, I didn't know you were back already."

"Yeah Mom, it rained pretty hard up in the campground, so we nixed the whole trip. What's for breakfast?"

"Melvin," his father blared, "have you been moving my things?"

"Nope."

"Melvin, I'm not playing with you."

Melvin, overconfident and waxing bold, shoots his dad an impudent look and begins to backtalk his father. Finished, and satisfied that he has fully expressed himself, Melvin then suddenly clams up and goes back to playing his video game.

"So disrespectful," mourns Robert.

"Oh Robert, leave him alone," whines Lumira, always standing up for the boy.

Melvin's flashy Mumbai trinket bracelet begins to feel hot and heavy, on his arm, like it's burning him. He wanted to take it off many different times, but he felt like it was working for him. It was getting him things and stuff, and most of all, the ladies. Plus, he was in the middle of this game, and he couldn't stop now.

Robert had been having bad dreams too. In the dreams, the walking stick became animated and the bird on it was also talking saying, *"Don't send her anything."* Robert would talk in his sleep. *"Don't send who?"* Then the bird would stop talking and not say another word. Robert chalked this up to his drinking, but instead of quitting alcohol, he'd take an extra Scotch every evening before bed;

now and it had been a year. His drinking was increasing, headed toward addiction.

Six months after Grandma had been dead and buried, this make-believe, make-shift, three-piece family *unit* was very content and happy. They had practically forgotten about Emily down in Virginia. Everyone thought they had what they wanted. Each thought they didn't have a care in the world and never would again. But as the months passed, it was now a full year later and there was the sound of bickering in the house, discord, tension, all the time. They each had lost respect for the others.

Eighteen months--, then nearly two years after Grandma's passing, these three couldn't stand one another, but something kept them together. Perhaps it was their heinous secret. Perhaps it was the money. Maybe it was distrust, they didn't dare let the other two out of their sight thinking they may run off with the rest of the money.

They took expensive and exotic vacations together, but they didn't enjoy any of them. Sure, they smiled for the pictures, that was for other people, that was for social media, but they did not enjoy each other's company anymore. That didn't make any of them think about Emily anymore either, they had even less care for her than before. Emily was the threat. Emily would be the undoing of all their enjoyment and freedom as far as they were concerned. In their minds, if not spoken aloud, Emily was the villain, not any of them, even though they were the ones who stole from her, not the other way around.

The *Unit* actually didn't like anyone anymore; they stopped liking people. They were becoming sociopaths, or they always were and were just now expressing their pathosis.

The money? They just spent and spent never considering that one day it would run out since none of them were doing anything much to replenish it – as if they could, anyway, at the rate they were spending. Even the parents temporarily forgot where money comes from and how to budget and hold on to what you have.

The cursed items they each brought back from Mumbai start showing signs of "claiming" them. In her dreams the raven was telling Lumira that they had to return to Mumbai. She didn't seem to know that she had to renew the contract and pay again. She knew or understood nothing about this level of evil even though she was that level of evil. Plus, she wasn't going to give that guy any more money, 20 thousand was enough, it was too much really. It wasn't too much money when she wanted that "spiritual" help, but now that she had gotten what she wanted, that was now too much money to pay for what she got.

Evil human nature: go figure.

Emily's dad had Grandma's phone since Grandma's memorial service, and just took it over, pretending to be Grandma to Emily. There was a little heart left in him; after all she was his firstborn and his daughter --, he used to be crazy about her. Robert thought that he couldn't leave her out there at university with nothing at all. He also had a very guilty conscience and was the one sending her money every now and then. He thought he was clever to use Grandma's phone and bank account and pretend it was from Grandma. After a year of indulging in what should have been Emily's money anyway, Robert began sending her the measly $250 per month for her rent, making sure she still wouldn't suddenly have enough to fly home and see that Grandma was gone and that the *Unit* was living large while she was barely living.

Robert's dreams began when the raven on his walking stick was telling him not to send her anything. *"Her"* was Emily, but Robert didn't know that. He dismissed every scotch-filled dream, especially when the walking stick became a talking stick. This level of evil requires that if you are stealing from someone you cannot give them any money; they must suffer. It looks like both Robert and Lumira were messing around in back alleys and in evil places where they never should have gone. They were out of their depth.

Melvin was clueless; he had no depth. Period. Walking or riding, day or night, he was just clueless and never should have stepped foot into an occultic or witchcraft parlor.

One by One – They start having accidents, Melvin totaled the Jeep, got a Range Rover and then totaled that only a few months later. His mom was so happy that he was okay and just bought him a third car, an Escalade.

There were unexplained illnesses that came out of nowhere. Lumira had small incidents in the kitchen, burns, cuts, scrapes. Robert had near misses and bumps and bruises in the garage when he was worshipping, I mean detailing his new cars.

They'd go to sleep fine and wake up sick. It caused them to spend time in Urgent Care. It caused them to spend money for meds and copays, but they didn't care, they felt rich and invincible as if nothing could conquer them. In three and a half years, they had blown through nearly three million dollars. Lumira had bought an expensive new home so if Emily had come home on a college break, she wouldn't have known where her "family" even lived. Every year Lumira and Robert would outright buy a new luxury vehicle for themselves. Lumira didn't care what she sold the old car for, but Robert collected all his. He has five cars now.

Also, in that time frame they each were having terrifying nightmares, but they weren't talking to one another very much, so no one knew, or even cared what the others were going through. They had lost natural affection for one another, if they ever had it in the first place. They considered themselves a family unit, they deceived themselves into thinking they were *close knit* because they all held a terrible secret, but really, they were more of an association of people, a criminal enterprise.

Jasmine has a way about her that people, like Melvin, just tell her things. For the last two years, Jane has heard about each incident from Jasmine. Jane said, "Sometimes, evil doesn't always need us to punish it." Jane loved Jasmine's uncanny way of searching out details online and was encouraging her to go to law school. Jasmine loved hearing legal stories and about Jane's recollections of her days on the bench. Jasmine didn't yet know it, but Jane was piecing together a crime, Not only that, those two would launch an online detective agency that would surpass the work of Nev and Kamie. Their agency would handle everything from broken hearts to divorces and even financial crimes, especially those against the elderly. Their tagline would be: *"Eventually, evil will punish itself."*

The Eyes Have It

The very day Emily sees the note attached to the back of the Bearer Bond; she knows that Grandma's demise was orchestrated. Before she can call Jasmine, before they plan to go see Judge Jane. Before Jane takes them to the North Shore, the magic that Lumira paid a spiritualist in a back alley in Mumbai starts to backfire on the *Unit*. It backfires before it didn't work; Emily was never supposed to know, but she knows. It backfires on the *Unit* because Emily was never supposed to know.

The next morning from the kitchen Lumira looks around their new house that she has decorated to perfection since they've now *arrived*. Her whole house is to her satisfaction. Each room is filled, if not overfilled with expensive but gaudy furniture. There is a pretentious staged air of wealth about the place.

On the wall above her favorite chair hangs the lotus-raven wall carving from Mumbai. Its red eyes catch the light, almost alive. It's as though it was ticking like a wind-up clock, but it wasn't a clock, it was more like a bomb. Something was about to happen. Lumira was clueless now. She smiled at her own accomplishments. The only thought in her mind is that Emily had been away for years and she thought soon she might convince Emily to stay away permanently. Plus, they had moved, and Emily didn't even know where the family now lived. Lumira chuckled an evil laugh to herself thinking she'd turn her mind to that soon enough.

Right now, as she made coffee and started preparing breakfast, Lumira turned her focus to trying to remember her dream from last night. She thought the bird was talking again but maybe she was dreaming about shopping, and she was buying slacks for Robert and Melvin. *Chinos*. That word kept echoing in her head, c*hinos*. It didn't make any sense, so she went on with her kitchen duties.

Robert had a vivid dream last night; in it he clearly heard, "She knows." But he didn't bother to know what that meant and just dismissed it.

Melvin, also dreamed, *She knows. She knows,* but he thought it was about a girl he was dating and cheating on--, as usual, so he was worried about what he would say to her when she confronted him. Then he laughed and sat down to play with his PS8 because he didn't care what she'd say, he would just get a new girlfriend. Maybe even two or three new girlfriends since he believed he had it like that.

Suddenly, in this TV perfect setting the front door burst open. It is the **POLICE** in tactical vests flooding in. They say one thing and then there is silence.

"You all are under arrest for conspiracy to commit murder... first-degree premeditated murder.

The raven's red gemstone eyes either glint or wink wickedly at that declaration.

Melvin is yanked up from the couch. As they cuff him, the thick silver-and-gold Mumbai bracelet bites into his wrist, leaving a red welt. He winces but says nothing. Then it suddenly broke, and fell in slow motion by some weird gravity, as if it was forced to let go. Its work was done. Melvin's chick magnet bracelet came a loose when he was handcuffed, and it lay on the floor, at one point that jewelry piece was inhabited by some strange force, but now--, it's dead.

Robert appears from the back coming to see what the noise is about. He's located his ornate carved walking stick—, brass raven head gleaming, and was just walking through the house with it as he often did.

An officer's hand goes to his weapon. "Drop it! Now!" Robert hesitates, in disbelief. "That's a weapon. Drop it, or I will shoot." *Robert's* grip tightens around this device that he's come to love and even need. This stick was either security or a reminder that he was always going to be making money in his businesses. But hearing those words and seeing the weapon drawn, he quickly lets it clatter to the floor. It hits the floor making both a hollow and heavy sound. It was other-worldly. Robert's hands go up until they are grabbed and cuffed behind him.

Lumira bursts out of the kitchen and stands by her favorite designer chair, the lotus-raven wall hanging looming above it. The carved red eyes catch the light, fixed on her as the cuffs click shut.

As they are handcuffed one by one including Lumira, the ring-leader, no one speaks, but they look at one another accusingly. The Unit is led out one by one, their cursed souvenirs staying behind — silent, watching. Mocking.

And Emily? She's miles away, safe, living the life Grandma meant her to have.

Yet, she knows.

The law might not have closed in if those curses hadn't backfired! Of course, the *unit* wouldn't have been so brazen to commit such acts except for the false courage they gained from the Mumbai artifacts. They went all the way to Mumbai thinking they were buying protection and power, but instead, they brought home the very things that would undo them.

It's like the curses didn't just backfire — they *cleared the way* for the truth to surface. Every bad choice they made left a trail, and every "souvenir" became a beacon pointing straight at their guilt.

And the best part? Emily never had to get her hands dirty. The *Unit* destroyed itself. Yes, the police came in with three sets of handcuffs, for the premeditated murder of Pearl Donovan.

CSI would return later to collect evidence, but until they did the carved lotus with the raven with the red eyes would watch over that house because Lumira brought it home when they cleared out her mother's house looking for valuables to liquidate before she illegally sold it.

Whether Lumira brought that Mumbai carving home as a trophy or a good luck charm, it backfired on her because those three were all found guilty as hell, and they all got the penalty they wanted for Grandma. But Grandma was never guilty. And, Grandma was never dead.

Guess the *Unit* fooled around and found out that you don't mess with Grandma.

For more tales of power, betrayal, and redemption read other books by Nia Zola and also tune in to her channel on You Tube, Very Rich stories at Africa Untold Tales.

Books by Nia Zola

The Prince Has a Big Snake, https://a.co/d/bpzUH2M

You may view the abbreviated You Tube video version of this story on the Africa Untold Tales

channel. It is entitled: *JANGO: The Scent of Trouble.*
https://www.youtube.com/watch?v=NMRlqv18_uM

Book: **The Bewitching of Jango**, https://a.co/d/b8m7EVz

There are other fine stories on that channel as well. https://www.youtube.com/@AfricaUntold-llc

www.ingramcontent.com/pod-product-compliance
Lightning Source LLC
Chambersburg PA
CBHW071131250626
47159CB00006B/2204